Oliver Twist

Oliver Twist

CHARLES DICKENS

Condensed and adapted by
W. T. Robinson

Illustrated by
Martin Hargreaves

Cover illustrated by
Tom Newsom

Plate colorization by
Jerry Dillingham

Dalmatian Press

The Dalmatian Press Great Classics for Children
have been adapted and illustrated with care and thought,
to introduce you to a world of famous authors, characters, ideas,
and stories that have been loved for generations.

Editor — Kathryn Knight
Creative Director — Gina Rhodes
And the entire classics project team of Dalmatian Press

OLIVER TWIST
Copyright © 2004 Dalmatian Press, LLC

The DALMATIAN PRESS name and logo are trademarks
of Dalmatian Press, LLC, Franklin, Tennessee 37067
No part of this book may be reproduced or copied in any form
without the written permission of Dalmatian Press.

ISBN: 1-40371-253-0 (M) 1-40370-794-4 (X)
13560

05 06 07 08 09 LBM 15 14 13 12 11 10 9 8 7 6 5 4 3

A note to the reader—

A classic story rests in your hands. The characters are famous. The tale is timeless.

This Great Classic for Children by Dalmatian Press has been carefully condensed and adapted from the original version (which you really *must* read when you're ready for every detail). We kept the well-known phrases for you. We kept the author's style. And we kept the important imagery and heart of the tale.

Literature is terrific fun! It encourages you to think. It helps you dream. It is full of heroes and villains, suspense and humor, adventure and wonder, and new ideas. It introduces you to writers who reach out across time to say: "Do you want to hear a story I wrote?"

Curl up and enjoy.

DALMATIAN PRESS
GREAT CLASSICS FOR CHILDREN

CONTENTS

CHARACTERS

AGNES FLEMING — mother of Oliver Twist

OLIVER TWIST — a poor orphan boy, born in a workhouse

OLD SALLY — a workhouse nurse

MRS. MANN — she runs the orphan work farm

MR. BUMBLE — a beadle, a parish official

MRS. CORNEY — she runs the workhouse

MR. SOWERBERRY — the undertaker, who takes Oliver in

MRS. SOWERBERRY — the undertaker's wife, a mean and hateful woman

NOAH CLAYPOLE — a mean young man (later known as Mr. Bolter) who works for Mr. Sowerberry

CHARLOTTE — a servant (later known as Mrs. Bolter) who works for Mrs. Sowerberry

LITTLE DICK — a poor young lad at the work farm

JACK DAWKINS — known as The Artful Dodger, a young pickpocket who works for Fagin

CHARACTERS

FAGIN — a ringleader of thieves and pickpockets

CHARLEY BATES — a thief who works for Fagin

BILL SIKES — a brutal robber and housebreaker

BULL'S-EYE — Bill Sikes's shaggy white dog

BET — a thief who works for Fagin

NANCY — Bill Sikes's girlfriend, who works for Fagin

TOBY CRACKIT — a housebreaker

MR. FANG — a cruel judge

MR. BROWNLOW — a kind old gentleman

MRS. BEDWIN — housekeeper to Mr. Brownlow

MR. GRIMWIG — a friend of Mr. Brownlow's

MONKS — a mysterious man who hates Oliver

MRS. MAYLIE — a lady who befriends Oliver

ROSE MAYLIE — Mrs. Maylie's niece... or is she?

DR. LOSBERNE — a doctor friend of Mrs. Maylie

CHAPTER ONE

A Lonely Childhood

In almost every town in England, large or small, there is one very old and plain building— a workhouse. People with no money (paupers, as they were called) and orphan children (with no parents to love them) were sent to these workhouses. Here they lived and worked under very poor conditions. The food was bad and the work was hard. The local church parish ran the workhouses through a group of men who served on a committee, called a parish board. It was *their* job to look after the workhouses and keep things in order.

In just such a workhouse, in a town not named,

a baby boy was born. A local doctor and an old nurse named Old Sally helped with the baby's birth.

The baby boy took a big breath, sneezed, and let out a loud cry. His mother lived just long enough to whisper something to the old nurse and then hold her baby in her arms and give him one kiss.

Pausing by the bed, the doctor said, "She was a good-looking girl. Where did she come from?"

"She was found lying in the street," replied Old Sally. "She must have walked a long way, for her shoes were worn to pieces. Where she came from or where she was going to, nobody knows."

"It's a sad story when a baby's mother dies and no father is around," said the doctor.

The child was left in the workhouse and given the name Oliver Twist. The names were just made up according to the alphabet. They needed a last name beginning with "T." Twist was as good as any. And so was Oliver.

The baby's father might have been a rich man or a beggar—nobody knew, for he could not be found. So the tiny child was an orphan who would be kept in the workhouse where he would never get the love and care a child needs. Instead, he would be made fun of and treated badly.

Before his first birthday, Oliver was sent to another home—a work farm, it was called. There, he and thirty more unwanted children were put into the care of Mrs. Mann. She was a mean woman who starved the children and stole most of the money which was supposed to be used to feed them.

A great many of the children died from poor care and lack of food. They were not washed or fed properly unless someone from the parish was coming to visit. Oliver Twist lived like this for eight years. He was a pale, thin child. Although he was small and weak from lack of food, he had a good heart and a strong spirit inside.

On his ninth birthday, poor Oliver was put into a dark basement with two other boys. They had been locked up, after a bad beating, for saying they were hungry. That very same morning, Mr. Bumble paid Mrs. Mann a surprise visit.

Now, Mr. Bumble was a round man with a hot temper. He had a job with the local parish board and was called a beadle. Mr. Bumble thought this was a rather grand title. (However, it was not quite as grand as he imagined.) This beadle thought *he* was important enough to act rudely—so he kicked and rattled the big metal gate of the work farm.

"Do you think this proper, Mrs. Mann, to keep a parish board member waiting?" he grumbled.

With great respect, Mrs. Mann took the man's hat and cane and placed them on a table.

Bumble told Mrs. Mann that Oliver Twist was now nine years old and ready to leave the farm and return to the workhouse. Soon, a freshly-scrubbed Oliver was led into the room. He was given a slice of bread, and a little brown cap was placed on his head. Then Mr. Bumble led him away from the awful home where not one kind word or look had ever brightened his day.

Before Mr. Bumble handed him over to Mrs. Corney, the woman who supervised the workhouse, he told Oliver that he was to appear before the parish board. Not having much of an idea of what *that* was, Oliver was not quite certain whether he ought to laugh or cry.

"Bow to the board," said Bumble, as he led the boy into a room where several men with powdered wigs sat around a meeting table.

Oliver was frightened at the sight of so many proper gentlemen. He brushed away two or three tears and looked around. The only board he saw was the long board of the table. So he bowed to *that*.

Mr. Bumble gave him a quick tap of his cane from behind, which made him cry.

"The boy is a fool," said one of the well-dressed gentleman in a fancy white coat.

Another asked, "Sir, you do know you've got no father or mother, and that you were brought up by the parish, don't you?"

"Yes, sir," replied Oliver, weeping bitterly.

"Well! You have come here to be educated and taught how to work for your pay. So you'll begin tomorrow morning at six o'clock!"

Oliver was hurried away to a huge room full of rough, hard beds. There he sobbed himself to sleep.

The workhouse was an awful place, to be sure. The only food Oliver and the other boys *ever* got was a watery cereal, called gruel, and no more. The copper bowls never needed washing. The boys polished them with their spoons—scraping up every last little bit. Then, they would sit staring at the empty pots with eager eyes, sucking their fingers.

The poor boys got weaker and weaker. After three months, the boys held a meeting to see which of them would walk up to the master after supper that evening—and ask for more food. They all drew straws—and Oliver lost.

The supper hour came. The master of the workhouse passed out the gruel. It was soon gone, and Oliver was still hungry. Slowly he walked up to the master, with his bowl and spoon in hand.

Oliver said, "Please, sir, I want some more."

The master could not believe what he had heard!

"What!?" he shouted.

"Please, sir," replied Oliver, "I want some *more.*"

The master, steaming with anger, aimed a blow at Oliver's head with his big spoon, and shrieked for Mr. Bumble.

The parish board met again and ordered that Oliver be put into a room by himself.

CHAPTER TWO

Oliver Escapes from the Coffins

For a week, Oliver remained a prisoner. He was forced to wash every morning under the water pump in a cold, stone yard. He was whipped every day. Oliver was used as an example of everything bad that the other boys should *not* be. He was forced to listen as they prayed that *they* would never be like *him*.

The board of gentlemen met to discuss what to do with Oliver Twist. They thought that perhaps he should be sent away on some small trading ship, headed to a good, unhealthy place. Meanwhile, Bumble asked the local undertaker if he needed a young boy to "train up" in his funeral business.

Indeed, he did.

The undertaker, a Mr. Sowerberry, met with the board for five minutes. It was agreed that Oliver should go to him that same evening. The boy heard the news of where he was to be sent, and said not a word. With nothing but a few things stuffed in a brown paper bag and his brown cap, Oliver followed Mr. Bumble to another place of suffering.

"Oh! That's the boy, is it? Come in here, Mrs. Sowerberry!" said the undertaker, calling to his wife. A short, unfriendly-looking woman came in from the back room. She glared at Oliver.

"He's very small," she snapped.

"But he'll grow, Mrs. Sowerberry."

"Ah! I guess he will," she fussed, "on our food and drink. Orphans always cost *more* to take care of than they're worth. Get downstairs, little bag o' bones."

With this, the undertaker's wife opened a side door and pushed Oliver down some steep stairs into a damp, dark room next to the coal cellar. There sat a messy-looking young lady in ragged clothes.

"Here, Charlotte," said Mrs. Sowerberry, "give this boy some of the cold scraps that were

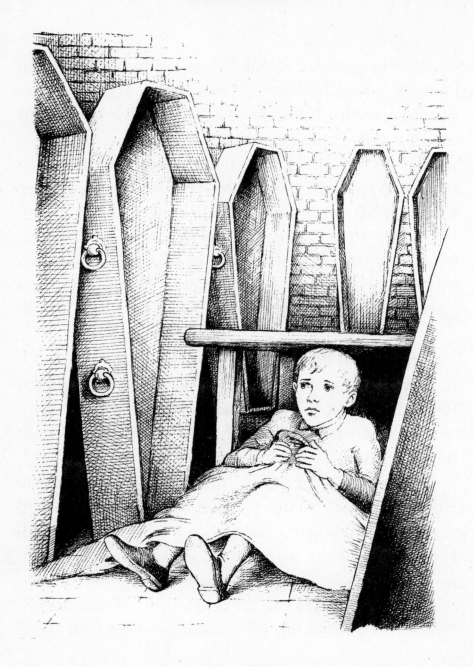

put out for the dog."

Oliver's mouth watered. He was hungry enough to eat anything. When he was finished, Mrs. Sowerberry pushed him into the room where coffins were stored.

"Your bed's under the counter. You don't mind sleeping among the coffins, I suppose? Well, it doesn't matter whether you do or don't, for you can't sleep anywhere else."

As he crawled into his narrow bed that night, the boy wished that it were his own coffin in a quiet graveyard, with tall grass waving gently above his head.

Oliver was awakened in the morning by a loud kicking at the outside of the shop door. Oliver unbolted the door and opened it slowly.

"I'm Mister Noah Claypole," said a mean-looking young man as he stepped through the door, "and *you're* under *me*. Get to work, you lazy workhouse boy." With this, he kicked Oliver and entered the shop, acting as if he were someone very important.

Noah Claypole was large-headed with small eyes. He was from a poor family, and he worked for Mr. Sowerberry. The neighborhood boys had

always made fun of him and his family. Now he had a chance to be mean to someone *else*. Here was an orphan-boy to boss around!

Oliver began to learn the funeral business. Mr. Sowerberry liked the look of Oliver's pale, sad face, so he dressed Oliver up to walk in the funeral marches. He had many chances to see the strength and courage with which people faced sorrow and death. This stuck in Oliver's mind. Oliver learned that the sad families were very thankful for the kindness and comfort he was able to give to them.

But he found no comfort within the Sowerberry house. For many months, Oliver put up with the mean Noah Claypole. Charlotte treated him badly because she saw Noah doing it. Mrs. Sowerberry disliked him just because Mr. Sowerberry seemed to like him—sometimes.

One day, Oliver and Noah Claypole were having supper when Noah decided to tease the young boy. He made several cruel remarks, but was not happy until he made Oliver cry.

"Yer know," said Noah, "yer mother was no good at all. And it's a lot better that she died when she did, or else she'd have been jailed or hung!"

Oliver jumped up, his face red with anger. He grabbed Noah by the throat and shook him until his teeth chattered in his head. With one heavy blow, Oliver knocked the young man to the ground.

"Help! Help! He's murdering me! Charlotte, help! Oliver has gone crazy!" cried Noah.

"Send for the police!" yelled Charlotte.

"Run and get the beadle, Noah," ordered Mrs. Sowerberry. "Mr. Bumble will know what to do with this awful boy!"

Mr. Bumble arrived and did not know what to do with the awful boy. The reports of Oliver's attack on Noah so worried Mr. Bumble that he spoke to Oliver through the door's keyhole. "Ain't you afraid of me? Ain't you a-trembling while I speak, sir?" said the beadle.

"No!" replied Oliver boldly.

"Mr. Bumble, he must be crazy to speak to you that way," said Mrs. Sowerberry.

"It's not that, ma'am," replied Mr. Bumble. "You've given him too much to eat. The only thing that can be done now is to leave him in the cellar for a while with no food. Then take him out and keep him on gruel all through the training."

When Mr. Sowerberry returned, he gave Oliver a sound beating. For the rest of the day, Oliver was shut up in the back kitchen with water and a slice of bread.

That evening, Oliver wept the saddest, loneliest tears he had ever wept. He made up his mind to run away. He tied up everything he owned in a handkerchief. Then, as the sun was just coming up the next morning, Oliver sneaked out into the street and started walking. He was not sure where he was going.

As he walked, he found himself near the big metal gate of the work farm where he had lived most of his childhood. He stopped and peeked into the garden. A child was working in one of the little beds of flowers. It was one of Oliver's old friends— a young lad—who looked up and saw Oliver.

"Hush, Little Dick!" said Oliver, as the boy ran to the gate. The small lad poked his thin arm between the rails to greet him. Little Dick had cried in cold cells with Oliver many times. "You mustn't say you saw me, Dick. I am running away. They treated me badly and beat me. Now, I am going to find a new life, some long way off. I don't know where. How white and sick-looking you are!"

"I heard the doctor tell them I was dying," replied the lad with a faint smile. "I am very glad to see you. But don't stop, don't stop!"

"I shall see you again, Dick. I know I shall! You will be well and happy!"

"I hope so," replied the child, putting his arms through the gate and flinging them round Oliver's neck.

"Good-bye, Oliver! Bless you!"

The blessing was from a young child's lips, but it was the first one that Oliver had ever been given in his whole life. He never forgot it.

CHAPTER THREE

Oliver Meets Fagin and His Band of Thieves

Oliver decided that he would go to London. Not even Mr. Bumble could find him there! Maybe somewhere in that big city someone would take a homeless boy off the streets.

It took him seven long, heart-breaking days to reach London. Early on the seventh morning, still outside of the city, Oliver sat crouched down on a step. He noticed that a boy was looking at him with great interest.

The boy was about his own age. He was one of the strangest-looking boys that Oliver had ever seen. He was dirty and he had small, sneaky eyes.

He wore a man's coat, which reached nearly to his heels, and he kept his hands stuffed in the pockets of his trousers. He wore a grown man's hat, which kept sliding to one side.

"Hullo! What's up?" the strange boy said.

"I am very hungry and tired," replied Oliver in tears. "I have been walking for seven days."

"Going to London?" asked the boy.

"Yes," replied Oliver.

"Got some place to stay?"

"No."

"Got any money?"

"No…"

"Never mind—you'll come along with me. I stay with a merry old gentleman who will feed you and take you in!"

The hungry young boy decided to accept the offer. When they stopped to get a bit of food, Oliver discovered that the boy's name was Jack Dawkins. His friends called him "The Artful Dodger" because he was such a sly, clever rascal.

Late that night they entered London. A dirtier or worse place Oliver had never seen. The streets were very narrow and muddy, and the air was filled with bad smells. There were children everywhere! Even at that time of night, they were crawling in and out of the doors or screaming from inside the homes and shops.

Oliver was ready to run away when the Dodger pushed open the door of an old house and pulled him inside. There stood a very old man with a cooking fork in his hand. His wrinkled face was hidden by a lot of dirty red hair. He seemed to be looking back and forth from the frying pan to a great number of silk

handkerchiefs hanging up nearby.

Seated round the table were four or five boys, none older than the Artful Dodger. They were smoking long clay pipes and acting more like men than boys.

"I've brought a pal. This is him, Fagin," said Jack Dawkins to the old man. "My friend—Oliver Twist."

Fagin peered at Oliver. Then he said, "Dodger, take the sausages off the stove and draw a stool near the fire for our new boy Oliver."

The boy ate his share and took a drink Fagin handed him. Afterward, he felt himself gently lifted onto a stuffed sack, and he sank into a deep sleep.

It was late the next morning when Oliver awoke. There was no other person in the room but the old man. He saw Fagin lift a small box from a hiding place in the floor. The old man's eyes glistened as he raised the lid and looked in. He took from the box an expensive gold watch, sparkling with gems. More beautiful jewelry filled the box. Fagin took out one small piece. There seemed to be some writing on it. Leaning back in his chair, he muttered, "What a fine thing it is… that dead men never tell!"

As the old man said these words, he looked over and saw Oliver. *The boy was staring at him!* Fagin closed the lid of the box with a loud crash and shouted, "What do you watch me for? What have you seen? Speak out, boy!"

"I wasn't able to sleep any longer, sir," replied Oliver quietly. "I am very sorry if I have bothered you."

"Did you see any of these pretty things, my dear?" said Fagin.

"Yes, sir," replied Oliver.

"Ah!" he said, turning rather pale. "They're mine, Oliver—all I have to live on in my old age. I just keep them in this box to keep them safe, that's all. But we'll forget you saw this, eh, my dear?"

He must spend all his money feeding these boys, thought Oliver. *He lives in such a dirty place for a rich man.*

Soon, the Dodger returned with a lad named Charley Bates.

"I hope you've been at work this morning, my dears," said Fagin to the two boys.

"Hard! As nails," cried the boys. They took some wallets and fancy handkerchiefs out of their pockets. Fagin looked them over, smiling.

"Hmm…" said Fagin. "Very nice, boys, but the stitching in these handkerchiefs will need to

be redone. We'll teach Oliver how to do that."

After they ate, Oliver watched as the old gentleman and the boys began playing a very strange game. Fagin filled his pockets with an eyeglasses case, a fancy pocket-handkerchief, and several other valuable things. He then trotted up and down the room with a stick, as if he were an old gentleman on the street with his walking cane. Sometimes he stopped at the fireplace, and sometimes at the door, making believe that he was staring into shop windows. All this time, Charley and Dodger followed around near him, getting out of his sight every time he turned.

At last, the Dodger stepped on the old man's toes. At the same time, Charley took the pocket-handkerchief and the glasses case from his pockets. But the old gentleman felt the hand in one of his pockets, so he cried out—and then the game began all over again.

After the game, two young ladies stopped by. One was named Bet and the other Nancy. They visited a bit, and then the Dodger and Bates and the two young ladies all left and went outside. The kindly Fagin gave them money to spend.

"Have they gone to work, sir?" asked Oliver.

"Yes, they have. Learn to be like them," said Fagin. "Do everything they ask of you and take their advice, especially the Dodger's. He'll be a great man one day, and he'll make you one, too. Is my handkerchief hanging out of my pocket, my dear?"

"Yes, sir," said Oliver.

"See if you can take it out—and mind you, I must not feel a thing!"

Oliver held up the bottom of the pocket with one hand (as he had seen the Dodger hold it), and lightly drew the handkerchief out with the other hand.

"Well, I never saw a sharper lad. Here's a coin for you. If you go on like this, you'll be the greatest man of the time," said Fagin.

Oliver couldn't understand how taking a handkerchief out of somebody's pocket could make anyone a great man.

CHAPTER FOUR

Oliver Is Trapped and Rescued

Oliver spent most of his days inside, either picking the stitched names off of Fagin's handkerchiefs or practicing Fagin's game. Before long, he began to beg the old gentleman to allow him to go out and work, too.

One morning, Fagin sent Oliver into the streets with Charley Bates and the Dodger, who were to teach him his new job. The two boys, doing their best to stay out of sight, sneaked up close behind a fine old gentleman. He was a wealthy-looking person with white hair and gold spectacles. He had picked up a book at one of the shops and stood there reading.

Soon, Oliver was shocked to see the Dodger plunge his hand into the fine old gentleman's pocket, pull out a handkerchief, and hand it to Charley Bates. Then they both went running round the corner at full speed!

In an instant the whole mystery of the handkerchiefs, the jewels, and Fagin filled Oliver's mind. He stood for a moment with the blood in all his veins tingling from terror. Confused and frightened, he ran.

As Oliver began to run, the old gentleman put his hand in his pocket and found his handkerchief missing. Turning quickly and seeing Oliver scurrying away so fast, he shouted, "Stop, thief!" and ran off after him, book in hand.

The Dodger and Charley saw Oliver run by them, and they, too, ran off, shouting, "Stop, thief! Stop, thief!"

Away they all ran, yelling, screaming, and knocking people down as they turned the corners. Even all the dogs started barking.

Terrified, Oliver ran to keep ahead of everybody chasing him. Then, *pow!* A sharp and clever punch knocked him from his feet. He looked up to see a man with a pale, twisted face,

staring very hard at him. The man turned and left as a crowd began to form. The fine old gentleman (whose handkerchief had been stolen) was among them.

A police officer made his way through the crowd and grabbed Oliver by the collar.

"It wasn't me, sir. It was two other boys," Oliver cried, clasping his hands and looking around.

"Don't hurt him," said the old gentleman, in a kind and tender voice.

Oliver was placed into a stone jail cell and searched. Nothing was found. The gentleman, named Mr. Brownlow, began to think Oliver was telling the truth. *There is something in that boy's face*, he thought, *something familiar that touches me. Can he be innocent?*

Mr. Brownlow tried to remember all the faces from his past. Something made him feel he had seen Oliver before. He could not think when or where it might have been.

Soon, the old gentleman and Oliver stood before a judge by the name of Fang—known for his cruelty. The police officer stated that he had captured the suspect, searched him and found

nothing on him. The judge would not listen to
Mr. Brownlow as he tried to explain things.

Judge Fang turned to Oliver. "What's your name?"

Oliver tried to reply, but couldn't talk. He felt

like he was going to faint. The whole room seemed to be turning round and round. He could not answer the question. Knowing that *no* reply would make Mr. Fang even angrier, the police officer tried to help, saying:

"He says his name's Tom White, your Honor."

At this point, Oliver raised his head, looked around, and asked for water.

"Stuff and nonsense!" said Mr. Fang. "Don't try to make a fool of me."

"I think he really *is* ill, your Honor," said the officer.

Oliver fainted and fell to the floor.

"Let him lie there," said Fang. "He'll soon be tired of that."

"How do you plan to deal with the case, sir?" asked the clerk as he bent over the boy.

"He is sentenced to three months at hard labor, of course. Clear the office!" ordered Mr. Fang.

A couple of men were getting ready to carry the boy to his jail cell when an older man rushed quickly toward the judge's bench.

"Clear the office!" cried Mr. Fang.

"I will speak!" cried the man. "I will not be turned away. I saw the pick-pocket! I saw it all."

The man went on: "I am the owner of the bookstore. Another boy did the robbery. I saw the whole thing, and I saw that *this* boy was shocked and surprised at what he saw."

"Then the boy is free to go. Clear the office!" roared Mr. Fang.

"Poor boy, poor boy!" said Mr. Brownlow, bending over him. "I'll take him with me."

The driver of the coach, which Mr. Brownlow hired, stopped before a neat house on a quiet, shady street. Oliver soon found himself in a soft, clean bed. He had never before been given such kindness and care. But Oliver was very ill, indeed, and fever raged through him for days and days.

Weak and pale, he finally awoke one morning as if from a bad dream. He raised himself up in the bed and looked around.

"Where am I? This is not the room I went to sleep in," he said.

"Hush, my dear," said an old lady softly. "You have been sick, very sick. Lie down again—that's it, little dear!"

With those words, the old lady gently placed Oliver's head upon the pillow. She looked so kindly and lovingly into his face that he could not

help placing his little hand in hers and pulling her arm around his neck.

"Mercy," said the old lady with tears in her eyes. "What a thankful little child it is. Pretty thing! What would his mother feel if she could see him now!"

"Perhaps she does see me," whispered Oliver, folding his hands together. "Perhaps she has sat by me. I almost feel as if she has. But heaven is a long way off, and they are too happy up there to come down to the bedside of a poor boy."

When he opened his eyes the next day, Oliver felt cheerful and happy. He was still too weak to walk, so the kind lady, Mrs. Bedwin the housekeeper, had him carried downstairs to her room. Oliver enjoyed sitting in Mrs. Bedwin's room. He particularly liked to look at a painting on the wall. It was a portrait of someone's face— a pretty, young woman.

"It is so pretty," he said, "but the eyes look so sad. Wherever I sit, they seem to follow me. It's as if she were alive and wanted to speak to me, but couldn't."

Just then, Mr. Brownlow entered the room.

"Poor boy, poor boy!" he said, clearing his

throat. "How do you feel, Tom White?"

"Very happy, sir, and very thankful for your goodness to me. But my name is Oliver, sir. Oliver Twist."

"Strange name!" said the old gentleman. "What made you tell the judge your name was White?"

"I never told him so, sir," returned Oliver, surprised at Mr. Brownlow's question.

This sounded so much like a fib that the old gentleman looked hard at Oliver's face. It was impossible to think he was lying. There was too much truth in his little eyes.

"Perhaps there was some mistake," said Mr. Brownlow, as he continued to stare at Oliver. He thought again how much Oliver's face reminded him of another face he had seen. He could not get it out of his mind. Then he looked up at the portrait above Oliver's head. He studied it—then stared again at the boy's face. The two faces looked almost alike! Mr. Brownlow let out such a sharp cry of wonder that Oliver fainted away out of fear.

CHAPTER FIVE

Oliver Is Safe–The Thieves Are Not

In another part of the city, the Dodger and Charley Bates were also fainting as they arrived home, but they were fainting from laughter. Charley was joking about the chase after poor Oliver. He laughed so hard that he woke Fagin.

"Where's Oliver?" said Fagin, grabbing the Dodger tightly by the collar.

"Why, the police have got him," he said.

Picking up a pot of stew, Fagin threw it at the boy's head, but missed. Instead, the stew splattered all over a stout man coming through the doorway, who demanded, "What's goin' on, Fagin?" Looking down beside him, the visitor added,

"Come in, you old mutt. Don't be sneaking around as if you was ashamed of your master! Come in!"

A white shaggy dog slinked into the room. His face was scratched and torn in twenty different places. The big man gave him a kick. The dog, whose name was Bull's-eye, seemed to be used to bad treatment. He curled himself up in a corner without making a sound.

"What are you up to? Treating the boys mean, you old crook?" said the big man, seating himself. He was a frightening sight. He was unshaven, dressed in dirty clothes, and had a black eye.

"Well, well, then—Bill Sikes," said Fagin. "You seem a little angry, Bill."

"Perhaps I am," replied Sikes. He told Fagin to give him a drink. "And mind you, don't poison it." This was said as a joke, but Fagin's face had an evil smile as he turned to the cupboard.

After swallowing a few drinks, Sikes listened to the story of Oliver's arrest in the street.

"I'm afraid," said Fagin, "that this boy will say something that will get us in trouble. The game may be up for a lot of people. It would come out worse for *you* than it would for *me*, my dear," he said to Sikes.

"If he hasn't told on us, and is in prison, there's nothing to worry about until he gets out," said Mr. Sikes, "and then he must be taken care of. You must get hold of him somehow."

Just then, Bet and Nancy entered the room.

"The very thing!" said Fagin. He went on to explain about Oliver to the two young ladies.

"You're the person to go to find out what's

become of the boy, Nancy," said Sikes. "Nobody knows you."

"I'll not go, Bill," said Nancy.

"She'll go, Fagin," said Sikes.

"No, she won't, Fagin," said Nancy.

"Yes, she will, Fagin," said Sikes.

And Mr. Sikes was right. Nancy finally was forced to go to the police and find out what she could about Oliver. She learned that a gentleman had carried Oliver away in a coach to his own home. The coach driver remembered the name of the street. Nancy hurried back to Fagin with the information.

"Oliver must be found," said Fagin. "If he hasn't blabbed about us to his new friends yet, we may still have time to close his mouth."

Meanwhile, Oliver was lying safe in a warm bed. He had quickly recovered from his faint. However, the old gentleman and Mrs. Bedwin were careful not to talk about the face in the painting.

These were happy days for Oliver—quiet, neat, and peaceful. Everybody was so kind and

gentle, it seemed like heaven itself. Just as soon as Oliver was strong enough to put his clothes on properly, Mr. Brownlow ordered a complete new suit, new cap, and a new pair of shoes for him.

Oliver asked Mrs. Bedwin to sell his old clothes and keep the money for herself. Oliver looked out of the parlor window and saw a peddler roll them up and walk away. Oliver happily thought he would *never* have to wear them again. They were truly sad rags to him.

About a week later, Mr. Brownlow called Oliver into his study. Oliver was scared when he saw the serious look on his face.

"Oh, don't tell me you are going to send me away, sir, please!" cried Oliver. "Don't turn me out to wander in the streets again. Let me stay here and be a servant. Don't send me back to the awful place I came from, please. Have mercy upon a poor boy, sir!"

"My dear child," said the fine old gentleman, feeling sorry for Oliver, "you need not be afraid that I will leave you all alone, unless you give me a reason."

"I never, never will, sir," promised Oliver.

"I hope not," said Mr. Brownlow. "Sad to say, I have been fooled before. But I trust you, and I am very interested in taking care of you. The people whom I have loved the most lie deep in their graves. But I still have my love for them in my heart."

He encouraged Oliver to always tell the truth, adding, "You shall always have a friend as long as I am alive."

At this moment, Mr. Brownlow's long-time friend, Mr. Grimwig, came through the door. He was a fat old gentleman, rather lame in one leg. He had a way of tipping his head to one side when he spoke, like a parrot.

"Look here! Do you see my leg? I slipped on an orange peeling left on my stairs. I would bet that orange peels will kill me some day. If I'm wrong, I'll eat my own head, sir!" said Mr. Grimwig.

(This was a promise Mr. Grimwig made after many things he said. It was silly enough, but it was even more silly because his head was so large. A man could hardly hope to eat it all in one meal!)

"I'll eat my head, sir!" repeated Mr. Grimwig, striking his walking stick upon the ground. "Hallo! What's that?" He looked at Oliver.

When Mr. Brownlow told him he didn't know much about the boy, Mr. Grimwig laughed.

"He is pulling a trick on you," he said. Then he asked if the housekeeper counted her silverware at night, to see if a tablespoon or two were ever missing.

"I'll swear to that boy's honesty with my life!" said Mr. Brownlow, knocking the table.

"And I'll swear he's fooling you, or I'll eat my own head!" said Mr. Grimwig.

Mrs. Bedwin came in then. She carried some books Mr. Brownlow had ordered that morning at the bookstore. A delivery boy had just brought them over.

"Stop the delivery boy, Mrs. Bedwin!" said Mr. Brownlow. "There are some other books to be taken back, too."

"Send Oliver with them," said Mr. Grimwig, with a sly smile. "He will be sure to deliver them safely, you know. Let's see if you really can trust him. Give him the money and see if he ever comes back."

"I won't be ten minutes, sir," said Oliver eagerly.

"Bless his sweet face!" said the old lady.

"Oh! You really expect him to come back, do you?" asked Mr. Grimwig. "The boy has a new suit of clothes, a set of valuable books under his

arm, and money in his pocket. He'll join his old friends, the thieves, and laugh at you. If ever that boy returns to this house, sir, I'll eat my head."

There the two friends sat—watching the clock—after Oliver left. The men sat in silence. They would have a long wait before they saw Oliver again.

CHAPTER SIX

Oliver Is Kidnapped

Bill Sikes and Nancy also sat in silence. They were in *The Three Cripples* inn where they often went for a drink. Before long, Fagin entered. He smiled and sat down at the table.

"Grin away," said Sikes, looking at him angrily. "Grin away. If they catch *me*, they'll catch *you* next. So you better take care of *me*!"

"Well, well, my dear," said Fagin, "I know all that. We *both* have reasons to find that boy, don't we?"

Sikes butted in, "Where is it? Hand over the money!"

"Yes, yes, Bill," replied Fagin, taking a small package from his pocket. Sikes snatched it from him and began to count the coins inside.

"This is all, is it?" asked Sikes. "This is all you got for those things I stole?"

"That's all," replied Fagin. "And now there's something you and Nancy need to do for *me*." He whispered something to them. They got up and were quickly on their way out the door.

Meanwhile, Oliver Twist was on his way to the bookstore. He was thinking how happy he ought to feel. But he also thought about how much he would give for only one look at poor Little Dick back at the orphan's work farm. Hungry and beaten, Dick might be weeping at that very moment. Oliver was startled from his thoughts by a young woman screaming out:

"Oh, my dear brother!"

Oliver started to turn to see what the matter was when he was stopped by a pair of arms thrown tight round his neck.

"Don't," cried Oliver, trying to get free. "Let go of me. I am not your brother. I haven't any sister, or father, or mother either. I'm an orphan."

Just then, he saw her face under her straw hat for the first time. "Why, it's Nancy!"

"What the devil's this?" said a big man,

bursting out of a shop, a shaggy white dog at his heels. "Young Oliver! Come home to your poor mother, you young dog! Come home right now!"

"I don't belong to you," cried Oliver, trying to get out of the man's powerful hold.

Weak, and scared by the dog as well as the man, Oliver could do nothing. They rushed him through the narrow streets. Bill Sikes ordered him to take hold of Nancy's hand. Bull's-eye led the way. Licking his lips, he looked at Oliver as if he wanted to get his teeth into the boy's throat.

Oliver had no idea where they were taking him. Bull's-eye came to a stop before the door of a shop that was closed and looked empty. But once inside, Oliver saw that it was not. It was Fagin's new hideout.

"Happy to see you looking so well, my dear," said Fagin, bowing. He noticed Oliver's new clothes. "The Dodger shall give you another suit, my dear, so you don't spoil that nice new one."

Fagin went through the scared boy's suit pockets. He grabbed the money which Mr. Brownlow had given Oliver.

"You can have those books," Fagin told Sikes.

"They belong to the old gentleman," said Oliver, wringing his hands. "The old lady—and all of them who were so kind to me—will think I stole from them. Have mercy upon me and send the books back!"

All of a sudden, Oliver ran wildly from the room, screaming for help. Bull's-eye leaped up to follow him.

Nancy shrieked, "Keep back the dog! He'll tear the boy to pieces!"

Bill Sikes pushed Nancy aside. Two of Fagin's boys returned, dragging Oliver between them. Fagin hit Oliver on his shoulders with a club and was raising it for a second swing when Nancy grabbed it from his hand.

"I wish I had been struck dead in the street before I brought him here," cried the girl (for a girl she was, being only seventeen). "Now, because of you, Fagin, he's a thief and a liar from now on. Isn't that enough, you bad old man? I stole for you when I was a child not half as old as him!" she said, pointing to Oliver. "I have been in this business for twelve years now. It is my way of life. The cold, wet, dirty streets have become my home. You are the wicked person that drove

me to them long ago and you will keep me there, day and night, till I die!"

The girl made a rush at Fagin, but Sikes stopped her.

Charley Bates led Oliver into the kitchen. Here, with bursts of laughter, he pulled out Oliver's same old suit of clothes—the *very same* sad rags that Oliver had asked Mrs. Bedwin to sell. Poor Oliver put on his old clothes as Bates closed the kitchen door behind him.

CHAPTER SEVEN

A Beadle Bumbles
Back into the Story

Unlike poor Oliver, Mr. Bumble the beadle was happy as could be that bright morning. He came to the big metal gate of Mrs. Mann's work farm for poor children. He held his head high—for he thought he was a man of great power and importance.

There's that foolish Bumble, thought Mrs. Mann as she went to open the gate. "Mr. Bumble, come into the parlor, sir."

Mr. Bumble proudly announced to Mrs. Mann that he was to make a very important trip to London. After giving Mrs. Mann her pay, he

listened to news of the children.

"And Little Dick. Isn't that boy any better?" asked Mr. Bumble.

Mrs. Mann shook her head.

"He's a sickly, bad-tempered child," said Mr. Bumble angrily. "Where is he?"

After some looking, Dick was found. His face was put under the pump, washed, and dried on Mrs. Mann's dress. Then he was brought to Mr. Bumble. The child was pale and thin, his cheeks were sunken, and his eyes large.

"Can't you look at the gentleman, you stubborn boy?" said Mrs. Mann.

The child quietly raised his eyes.

"You have everything you need, I'm sure," said Bumble.

"I should like… I should like for someone to write a few words down for me and keep it until after I am laid in the ground."

"What do you mean, child?"

"I should like to leave my dear love in a note to poor Oliver Twist. I'd like to let him know how often I have sat by myself and cried to think of his wandering about in the dark nights with nobody to help him. And I should like to tell him," said the child, pressing his small hands together, "that I was glad to die when I was very young. If I had lived to be a man, and had grown old, my little sister who is in heaven might forget me. It would be so much happier if we were both children there together."

Mr. Bumble looked at the little boy as if he could not believe what he heard. He cared nothing about Little Dick. Turning to the woman, he said, "They're all in it together, Mrs. Mann. That Oliver Twist is to blame for all of this. He ruined them all. They have no respect! Take him away, ma'am! This must be reported to the board!"

Dick was immediately taken away and locked up in the dark basement.

At six o'clock the next morning, Mr. Bumble left for London. By evening, he was enjoying a rather large meal at an inn and was reading the newspaper, when suddenly he noticed a notice in the paper.

REWARD FOR LOST BOY
OLIVER TWIST

The notice went on to describe Oliver and how he had come to be lost. Mr. Brownlow's name and address were given at the bottom as the person offering the reward. Mr. Bumble did not even finish his meal. He rushed out of the inn and headed straight for Brownlow's house.

"Is Mr. Brownlow at home?" he asked of the girl who opened the door.

He was shown into the little library where Mrs. Bedwin, Mr. Brownlow and his friend Mr. Grimwig were sitting. Grimwig whispered to Brownlow, "If *he's* not a beadle—a parish toady—

I'll eat my head."

"I've come about the notice in the paper," said Bumble.

"Well, what do you know of Oliver?" Mr. Brownlow asked.

Mr. Bumble said that Oliver was an orphan, born of worthless, poor parents. He told Mr. Brownlow that Oliver had been a bad child from the day he was born and had always been sneaky, ungrateful and hateful. He went on and on about Oliver, making him out to be a much worse child than he ever was. Mr. Bumble laid some papers on the table that proved he was a parish beadle—and therefore *must* be telling the truth. Folding his arms and acting quite proud of himself, Bumble waited to see what Mr. Brownlow would have to say.

"I fear it must all be too true," said the old gentleman sadly, handing Bumble some coins for his trouble. "That boy Oliver fooled us, Mrs. Bedwin. He is not the boy we thought he was."

"I never will believe it, sir," replied the old lady firmly. "Never!"

There were sad hearts at Mr. Brownlow's that night.

A Robbery Is Planned

There was another sad heart in London that evening. Oliver cried as he thought of his kind friends at the Brownlow home. It was better that he did not know what Mr. Bumble had told them, or his heart might have been completely broken.

The next day, Fagin tried to teach Oliver a lesson. He told him of another young boy, a boy Fagin had tried to take care of. That boy had broken his trust with Fagin by telling the police what he knew. The boy had unfortunately been hanged by the police. With tears in his eyes, Fagin said that the young man had caused his own problems when he made the mistake of talking to the police. Fagin ended the story by telling Oliver what it was like to be hanged by the neck until dead.

All of the time he was talking to Oliver, Fagin seemed as kind and friendly as could be. He said he *never* wanted to see such a thing happen to Oliver Twist. Then, he went out and locked Oliver in the room.

After a week or so, Fagin left the door of the room unlocked. Oliver was at last free to wander around the house. Often, feeling so alone, he would crouch down in the corner next to the street door to be as close to living people as he could. He would remain there, listening and counting the hours until Fagin or the boys returned.

One afternoon, the Dodger and Charley Bates came into Oliver's room. The Dodger looked over to Bates and said, "What a pity Oliver isn't a thief!"

"Yes, why don't you go to work for Fagin, Oliver?" asked Charley Bates.

"And make your fortune!" added the Dodger with a grin.

"I could not do that. I would rather go someplace else to live," Oliver said.

"You'd rather go and live off your friends, then?" said Dodger, "Well, *I* couldn't do that."

"But you can leave your friends in the street, though, can't you?" said Oliver with a little smile, "and let them be arrested for what *you* did."

From that day on, Oliver was almost never left alone. The two boys made sure they were with him. They played the old game of Pick-the-Pocket with Fagin every day. At other times, the old man would tell them stories of robberies he had taken part in during his younger days. Oliver could not help laughing sometimes.

The sly Fagin was slowly leading Oliver into his trap. By keeping him busy with the games and the boys, he kept Oliver from thinking of anything else. He was filling Oliver's mind and soul with evil things and ideas, which he hoped would turn Oliver into a thief.

One day, Fagin told Sikes about a house he had learned of "from a new friend." The friend had told him of things worth stealing from this house. The robbery was planned with another thief named Toby Crackit. They needed

someone small to crawl through a window. Fagin decided to put Oliver to work since he was just the right size. Nancy, who stayed with Bill Sikes, went over to get Oliver that evening.

"You are to go with me," Nancy said. Looking nervously around to be sure they were alone, she warned Oliver: "If ever you are to escape from here, this is not the time. Remember this! I am your friend, but don't make me suffer for it. So, keep quiet for now. If you say a word about this, Bill Sikes will beat me."

They left for Sikes's hideout. When they arrived, Sikes spoke roughly to Oliver. Then the evil robber pulled out a gun and said he would use it if there was any trouble.

Late that evening, Sikes and Crackit sneaked off with Oliver to a large house. Toby Crackit had two pistols and gave Sikes a stick to carry. Crackit put out his hand to Oliver.

"Now then!" he said. The child, without thinking, put his own little hand into Crackit's. And then, for the first time, Oliver realized what was about to take place. Housebreaking! Robbery! Maybe even murder! He sank to his knees.

"Oh! Please let me go!" cried Oliver. "Let me run away and die in the fields. Oh! Pray have mercy on me, and do not make me steal!"

The men refused his pleas and Crackit dragged Oliver along behind him. Sikes pointed to a tiny window, just the right size for Oliver.

Oliver felt helpless. He made up his mind to somehow let the owners of the house know what was happening—even if it meant his death. He climbed through the window. Once inside the house, he opened a door for Sikes and Crackit.

Oliver started to make a dash to warn someone. Sikes saw him and shouted out! Then a cry came from upstairs! Oliver stood there like a frightened animal. He didn't know whether to stay or run. There was another cry from upstairs, and a light appeared. Two men, frightened and half-dressed, came to the top of the stairs. There was a *flash*! and a loud noise!

"They've shot him," called Sikes. "Quick! The boy is bleeding!"

Sikes grabbed Oliver and ran out of the house. Oliver could hear shouts behind him. Someone was chasing them. Then he fainted and heard no more.

CHAPTER NINE

A Secret Never Dies

Outside London one cold evening, the matron who ran the workhouse sat by a cozy fire in her own cheerful little room. She was Mrs. Corney, a widow. She had just tasted her first sip of tea when she heard a soft tap at the door.

"Come in," she said sharply. "What's wrong now?"

"At your service, ma'am," said Mr. Bumble.

Mrs. Corney jumped up at once and began making him some tea.

"Care for something sweet, Mr. Bumble?" asked the matron.

"Very sweet, indeed, ma'am," replied Mr. Bumble. He looked right at Mrs. Corney as he said this. If ever a parish beadle could be tender, Mr. Bumble acted tender at that moment. In time, he brought his chair close. He drank his tea to the last drop, finished a piece of toast, wiped his lips, and then kissed the flustered woman.

"Mr. Bumble!" she giggled, just as there came a knock at the door of her room.

"If you please, mistress," said a wrinkled old woman, "Old Sally is a-going fast. But she says she can't die in peace until you come."

Mrs. Corney went upstairs, mumbling unkind remarks about old women who couldn't even die without her. Mr. Bumble stayed in the room.

While Mrs. Corney was gone, Mr. Bumble had a close look around her room. He opened closets, counted the silver teaspoons, and closely checked a milk pitcher to make sure it was real silver. Then, making himself comfortable in front of the fire, he studied all the furniture and figured up what it might be worth.

Upstairs, Mrs. Corney and two old pauper women bent over poor Old Sally.

"Come here! Nearer! Let me whisper in your ear," the dying woman said. She reached out and held Mrs. Corney by the arm. She was about to speak when she saw the two other women leaning forward.

"Send them away," said the woman. "Hurry!"

Mrs. Corney sent them out of the room.

"Now listen to me," said the dying woman. "In this very room, in this very bed, I once nursed a pretty young girl. She gave birth to a boy and died."

"What about her?" said Mrs. Corney.

Sitting right up in the bed, the dying woman cried, "I robbed her! She wasn't cold. I tell you, her body wasn't even cold when I stole it!"

"Stole *what*, for heaven's sake?" cried Mrs. Corney.

"Gold!" said the woman as she fell back.

"Go on. Who was the mother? When was this?"

"She asked me to keep it safe," groaned the woman, "and trusted me. And the poor child… Maybe they would have treated him better if they had known it all! The mother whispered in my ear that if her baby was born alive and grew older, the day might come when he could be proud of his mother. She could have sold the gold for food—but no! She had saved it for the baby! And she trusted me. He might have had a different life, but I stole all he had."

"The boy's name?" Mrs. Corney was very interested now.

"He grew to look so like her. They called him *Oliver*," replied the woman feebly. "The gold I stole was—"

Mrs. Corney quickly put her ear to the old woman's mouth, but drew back. Old Sally fell back on the bed and died. Her hand dropped from Mrs. Corney's arm and fell open.

Mrs. Corney took a small piece of paper from the hand and quickly put it in her apron pocket. Looking around, she turned and hurried out the door, brushing past the two old women as she left.

CHAPTER TEN

Fagin's Secret Meeting

Toby Crackit had gone to Fagin's house after he and Sikes had made their escape. He did not like having to tell Fagin that the robbery had failed and Oliver had been shot.

"They were close to catching us, so we left the young boy lying in a ditch. I don't know if he was alive or dead."

Fagin listened to no more. He gave a loud yell, rushed from the house, and ran into the streets. Once more he had lost Oliver!

Fagin stumbled through the town, wild from hearing Crackit's words. He had a *secret reason* for wanting the boy. He hurried to *The Three Cripples,* went to the innkeeper and asked, "Will he be here tonight?"

"Monks, you mean?" the owner of the inn asked.

"Yes! Tell him I came here to see him. Tell him he *must* come to me tomorrow. Don't say a thing about this," warned Fagin, walking out the door.

He stopped a carriage and paid the driver to take him to Mr. Sikes's hideout. Nancy was there

alone, her head on the table, crying. Fagin thought she was crying for the boy.

"Poor Oliver," said Fagin. "Poor little child! Left in a ditch! Nancy, just think of that poor boy!"

"The child," said the girl, suddenly looking up, "is better where he is than with *us*. And as long as no harm comes to Bill from it, I hope he *does* lie dead in the ditch."

"What!" cried Fagin, who could not believe what he had heard.

"I shall be glad to have him out of my sight— and to know that the worst is over. Just seeing that sweet boy makes me hate myself—and all of you," sobbed the girl.

"That boy means a great deal to *me*, too," cried Fagin. "Why, he's worth hundreds to me…" Fagin realized he was saying too much. "But you never mind what I said just now, Nancy. Yes, my dear?" Fagin's eyes looked wild as he hurried out the door.

———————

Fagin had reached the corner of his own street when a dark figure stepped out of the shadows. He was a tall, well-dressed young man, but his face was pale and twisted. His eyes were deeply set and his mouth turned up on one side.

"Fagin!" the figure whispered.

"Monks!" Fagin whispered back. He waved his arm at the strange man and led the way to his hideout. Safely inside, they began talking about the robbery.

"I gave you good information," said Monks. "But I tell you again, it was badly planned. You used the boy! Why didn't you just keep the boy here and make a pick-pocket out of him right away? He would have been arrested within a year, put in prison, and maybe sent safely out of the country—maybe for life!"

"That wouldn't have done *me* much good. I need to get *some* use out of the boy. But he just won't turn bad, I tell you. He's not like the other boys," said Fagin weakly. "Well, you know… you saw for yourself when he got caught for pick-pocketing with Dodger and Bates."

The strange man with the pale, twisted face glared at Fagin. "Never mind all that! You know what I want. I don't care about your business. I care about being rid of that boy for good. I have

different reasons than you for wanting that boy's mouth shut."

Then Fagin hunched forward and said quietly, "You should thank *me* that you ever found him to begin with. If you hadn't knocked him down that day for the police, you never would have recognized his face and started asking about the boy. You never would have found out he was the one you had been searching for..."

"Enough!" snarled Monks. "You must get him back and turn him bad! He could ruin everything for me!"

Suddenly Monks looked out the window.

"What's that?" he whispered.

"Where?" said Fagin.

"That shadow! I thought I saw the shadow of a woman in a cloak and bonnet—like a breath of air passing by."

Fagin rushed from the room, candle in hand, but found nothing. Monks decided he must have been seeing things that weren't there.

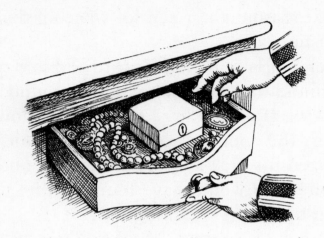

CHAPTER ELEVEN

Love Blooms in a Workhouse– and a Boy Is Left in a Ditch

Mr. Bumble had counted the silverware and figured out the value of Mrs. Corney's furniture. In fact, he did this many times. Then he began to think that it was time for her to return from Old Sally's deathbed. Since he heard nothing, he took one last peep into the drawers of her dresser. After finding some jewelry and a locked box in which coins rattled around, he thought it might be time that he had a *wife*.

He was proudly looking at himself in the mirror when Mrs. Corney scurried into the room.

"Oh, Mr. Bumble!" cried the lady, "I have

been so upset!" She batted her eyes. "It's such a comfort to have you here."

Nothing else was said for a minute or two.

"This *is* a very comfortable room, ma'am," said Mr. Bumble, looking round.

"It's a bit much for one person," murmured the lady.

"But not for two, Mrs. Corney," said Mr. Bumble in a soft voice.

Mrs. Corney dropped her head when Bumble said this. She sank into Mr. Bumble's arms as he gave her a kiss on the nose.

"Such parish perfection!" sighed Mr. Bumble. "You know that the master of the workhouse is quite ill. His death will leave that important job open—for me. Oh, Mrs. Corney, what a fine time to join our hearts in the same house!"

The workhouse matron threw her arms around Bumble's neck and called him "a darling duck."

>─┤◆>─O─<◆├─<

Mr. Bumble stopped at Mr. Sowerberry's on the way home and ordered a coffin for Old Sally.

>─┤◆>─O─<◆├─<

When Sikes and Crackit had decided to make a run for it after the failed robbery, they had dropped Oliver in a ditch. Some house servants with dogs had chased the robbers into the field, but soon gave up and returned to the house.

Oliver awoke early in the morning. His head was dizzy and he staggered back and forth. He spotted a house and stumbled toward it—only to see that this was the very house they had tried to rob. Nevertheless, he made his way to the front door.

Inside the house, the butler, Mr. Giles, and a handyman named Brittles were having tea in the kitchen. They had taken part in the chase the night before. Mr. Giles was telling some of the other servants the exciting story when a sound was heard on the front porch. The cook and housemaid screamed.

"It was a knock," said Mr. Giles, trying to stay calm. "Open the door, somebody."

Nobody moved.

Mr. Giles ordered Brittles to open the door. There stood poor little Oliver Twist, his arm bleeding. He looked up at them with sad, tired eyes.

"A boy! He's one of the robbers."

Moving to the foot of the stairs, Giles shouted, "Here he is, ma'am! Here's one of the thieves! I shot him myself and he's bleeding. Won't you come and take one look at him?"

"Not now," replied a lady's voice from upstairs. "Poor fellow! Treat him kindly, Giles, and see if you can find the doctor."

CHAPTER TWELVE

Fortune Finally Smiles on Oliver

The next morning, the two ladies of the house sat having a delicious breakfast. Mrs. Maylie, a proper older woman, sat across from her niece, Rose, a beautiful teen-age girl with a cheerful, happy smile.

At this moment, a carriage drove up to the garden. Out jumped a stout gentleman. It was Dr. Losberne, a local doctor and good friend of the family. He was shocked to hear of the robbery, but Rose was more worried about the patient. "There is a poor wounded thief upstairs whom you must see," she told the doctor.

"I understand that you did the shooting,

Giles," said the doctor.

Mr. Giles said that he was proud to have helped, and led the doctor upstairs to examine Oliver. When the doctor returned downstairs, he asked Mrs. Maylie if she had yet seen the thief.

"No," replied the old lady.

"I think you and Rose should come with me and have a look at him."

When they entered the room, the doctor gently drew back the covers of the bed. There the women saw just a tiny, wounded child, worn out from pain, in a deep sleep.

"What can this mean?" exclaimed the older lady. "This poor child could never have been a robber."

"But even if he *has* been wicked," said Rose, "think how *young* he is."

That evening, Oliver told them all about himself and what had happened to him. It was a sad story to hear in the darkened room.

Oliver gradually became stronger and happier under the care of Mrs. Maylie, Rose, and the kind-hearted Dr. Losberne. His arm was almost healed. In words of tearful thanks, he said how deeply he felt the goodness of the two sweet ladies. Oliver also wanted just as much to show

his thanks to Mr. Brownlow and Mrs. Bedwin. Dr. Losberne went to call on Mr. Brownlow, but learned that they had left town for the West Indies. This saddened Oliver, but he was still very happy with Mrs. Maylie and Rose.

Mrs. Maylie and Rose grew to love Oliver more each day. It was a peaceful, happy springtime for Oliver. His days with Mrs. Maylie were happy and hopeful. He and Rose were as close as blood relatives. As spring turned to summer, Dr. Losberne taught Oliver to write and gave him good books to read. Oliver became strong and healthy. But not everyone was as lucky.

One morning Rose woke up with a high fever. As the illness grew worse, Mrs. Maylie wrote a letter to the doctor and asked Oliver to take it to a nearby inn and give it to someone who would deliver it. Oliver was glad to help.

After giving the letter to a messenger at the inn, Oliver bumped into a tall man in a cloak, and fell to the street. Oliver picked himself up and said he was sorry. The stranger, a young man, stared at him with large, dark eyes. His ugly pale face grew paler and he began shouting and cursing at the boy. Then the man's mouth began to twist up and he suddenly fell to the ground in a fit. Oliver hurried home and told Mrs. Maylie of the awful man with the fit. But soon his thoughts and prayers turned to his sick friend Rose.

Several days and many prayers later, Rose was out of danger and feeling better. Mrs. Maylie's son Harry came from a long way off when he heard that Rose was sick. He told his mother how much he loved Rose and wanted to marry her. Mrs. Maylie told her son that she knew Rose loved him but that she could never marry him. Mrs. Maylie did not know Rose's true background—as she had taken the girl in when she was small. She could never allow her son to marry a girl (even a girl she called her niece) who had no family background.

One lazy summer day about a week later, Oliver sat reading and fell into a light sleep. He thought he was in a dream and that he was in Fagin's house again. He seemed to see the old, red-haired thief pointing at him and whispering to a tall, younger man. Suddenly he awoke, trembling with fear.

There at the window stood Fagin! And beside him was the scowling man with the pale, twisted

face who had cursed at him at the inn! Oliver screamed for help.

Oliver told Dr. Losberne what he saw and what the men looked like. When no clues of any kind could be found outside the window, Oliver began to think it really *was* all just a dream. He tried to forget it and enjoy his happy life.

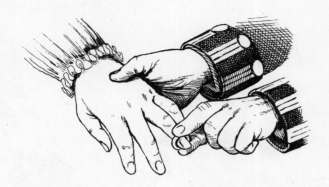

CHAPTER THIRTEEN

A Strange Twist of Events

Mr. Bumble married Mrs. Corney, and was now master of the workhouse. There were times when he and his new wife did not get along too well. One day after an argument with her, he went into town for some peace and quiet. There, a stranger stopped him.

The stranger knew of Bumble, and was interested in Oliver Twist. He wanted to find the old woman who had helped the doctor when Oliver was born. Mr. Bumble was sly and thought he saw a way to make a little money. He told the man that Old Sally was already dead, but that there had been a woman with her when she died.

"How can I find her?" said the stranger.

"I'm the only one who can find her for you," said Mr. Bumble.

They agreed to meet the next evening. The stranger gave Bumble an address.

Mr. Bumble asked, "Whom should I ask for?"

"Monks!" said the man.

Mr. Bumble returned the next evening, with his wife, to the address he had been given. It was a house built right over the river. Monks opened the door and showed them in. His face was twisted and had turned a pale purple.

"I have fits now and then," said Monks, noticing their surprise at his looks.

All three took a seat. Monks turned toward Mrs. Bumble. "What information do you have?"

"How much will you pay me for it?" asked the woman.

He put a large amount of money on the table. "Now, let's hear your story."

Mrs. Bumble began. "I was with the workhouse nurse—Old Sally—when she died. With her last few breaths she told me that many years ago she had been the nurse at the birth of this boy, Oliver. It seems Oliver's mother died right after he was born. But before the mother died, she gave something to the nurse and asked her to keep it for her son's sake. She said that someday it might make him proud of her and help to give him a better life."

"Go on! Go on!" cried Monks.

"Well, the old nurse told me that she had stolen what the young mother had given her. Just as she was trying to tell me what this thing was, she died. When her hand reached out to me as she took her last breath, I took a small slip of paper from her hand."

"I'll tear the life out of you both if I don't find out what it was!" Monks' face grew red as a beet.

"It was a pawnbroker's ticket."

"What did she pawn?" asked Monks quickly.

"This," replied Mrs. Bumble. She threw a small bag upon the table. Monks tore it open. It contained a gold locket with two locks of hair, and a plain gold wedding ring. The word "Agnes" was written on the inside of the ring with a blank space left for the last name. There was also a date—a year before Oliver's birth date.

"And this is all?" said Monks.

"That's all," said Mrs. Bumble. "I took the

ticket to the pawnshop, paid the money to buy it back, and this is what I was given."

"Does anyone else know about this? Anyone?"

"No. Just the three of us. I was alone with the old nurse when she died."

Suddenly Monks jumped up and pushed the table away. He opened a trap door in the floor beside Mr. Bumble's foot. Violent river water rushed by beneath them. Monks tied the ring and locket in a handkerchief, along with a heavy rock, and tossed it into the swift dark water.

"You'll say nothing about this to anyone, ever!" Monks snarled. "Get away from here as fast as you can."

CHAPTER FOURTEEN

A Thorn Seeks a Rose

Mr. Bill Sikes's luck had turned bad. He had moved to a filthy new hideout. A visit from Fagin only made him angrier. Fagin owed him money and he hadn't brought it with him. Sikes ordered Nancy to follow Fagin home to get his money.

While Nancy was waiting for the old villain to count out Bill's money, a visitor came to Fagin's hideout. Nancy heard a familiar voice. It was Monks'.

The two men went up the stairs to talk alone, but Nancy listened at the door. When they returned, she had her bonnet and shawl on, ready to leave. She was scared to death by what she had heard.

"Why, Nance," said Fagin as he placed the coins in her hand, "how pale you are!"

At home, Nancy could not hide her fear and nervousness. Bill did not trust her and began to watch her closely. One night, she secretly put a sleeping potion in his drink and hurried out.

She ran on and on to a little hotel in a nice part of the city. She told the clerk that she had an important message to deliver to someone at the hotel. Finally, Rose Maylie walked into the room where Nancy had been waiting. Here the two young ladies—both about the same age, but so very different—faced each other.

"Sit down," said Rose, in a kind voice. "If you are sick or need money I shall be truly glad to help you if I can."

"No," said Nancy. "I'll stand. I am about to put my life and the lives of others in danger. I am the girl that kidnapped Oliver Twist from Mr. Brownlow many months ago."

"You?" asked Rose. "Oliver has spoken of…"

"I am the woman you have heard of that lives among the thieves. Be thankful, dear lady, that *you* had someone to care for you in your childhood. Be thankful that *you* have never known cold and

hunger. I have lived in the streets, and I will die in the streets."

"I pity you!" said Rose. "It pains my heart to hear you!"

"Heaven bless you for your goodness. I have run away from those who would murder me if they knew I was here. Do you know a man named Monks?"

"No," Rose answered.

"He knows *you*," Nancy replied, "and knew you were *here* at this hotel. He's been a-spying on your house and watching where you go. That's how I knew where to find you.

"Several months ago, Monks came to Fagin— they did not know I was outside—and I overheard what this strange Monks said. Somehow he had recognized Oliver on the street when the boy was picked up by a policeman. He went to Fagin and told him he'd pay him a lot of money to find the boy and get him back. Then he said he'd pay him even *more* if he turned Oliver into a thief and a criminal. He did not say why... I know they have been meeting—in secret! Last night, Monks came again while I was at Fagin's—and I heard every word.

"Monks said the only proof of who Oliver *really is* lies at the bottom of the river. They laughed about trying to get the boy arrested for some crime and put in jail. Then, Monks said that Oliver was his *younger brother*. He hates Oliver, though I don't know why."

"His brother!" cried Rose. "But what can I do? I believe what you say. I want to help. Let me save you from the life you're living. I can make sure you go to a safe place."

"Lady," cried the girl, falling to her knees, "dear, sweet, angel lady, it is too late, too late!"

"But what can I do, then, with what you have told me? How am I to help Oliver?"

"Surely you know a kind gentleman you can tell—*someone* who could help," Nancy added with a hopeful face.

"Perhaps," said Rose, in thought. "But where can I find you again when I need to?"

"Every Sunday night, from eleven until the clock strikes twelve," said the girl, "I will walk on London Bridge—if I am alive. If you *must* find me, look for me there."

"Will you take some money from me, to help you until we meet again?" Rose asked.

"Not a penny," replied the girl, waving her hand. "It will be enough for me if what I have done by coming here somehow makes up for the kind of life I've lived. Bless you, sweet lady!"

><+>·⊙·<+><

Rose was sitting in her room going over Nancy's words. Rose needed help, but whom could she tell? She thought of Dr. Losberne, but decided he would tell the police, and that would get Nancy in trouble. Harry, the man she loved? No. But who? She was thinking about this when Oliver came through the front door, very excited.

"I have seen the old gentleman— *Mr. Brownlow*!" shouted Oliver.

While he had been out with Giles, Oliver had seen Mr. Brownlow get out of a coach and enter a house. Within five minutes, Oliver and Rose were on their way to that house.

When they got there, Rose told the servant who she was and asked to see Mr. Brownlow right away. The old gentleman was with Mr. Grimwig when he invited Rose to have a seat.

"Sir," said Rose, "I'm here because you have

shown great kindness to a very dear young friend of mine. You knew him as Oliver Twist."

Mr. Grimwig let out a long, deep whistle. Mr. Brownlow was also surprised.

"If you know things about that child, please tell me," said Brownlow.

"A bad one! I'll eat my head if he is not a bad child," growled Mr. Grimwig.

"He is a *good* child with a warm heart," said Rose. She told Mr. Brownlow of all that had happened to Oliver since he had left his house.

"But, where is he?" said the old gentleman.

"He is waiting outside," replied Rose.

Mr. Brownlow flew out of the room and returned with Oliver's hand in his own. Ringing the servant-bell, he said, "There is somebody else who should not be forgotten. Send Mrs. Bedwin here, if you please."

The old lady was still digging in her purse for her glasses when Oliver jumped into her arms.

CHAPTER FIFTEEN

We Learn of Noah, Charlotte, and the Dodger

On the very same night that Nancy met with Rose, two rather bad characters arrived in London. They were Noah Claypole and Charlotte, who had worked with the undertaker, Mr. Sowerberry. Charlotte could hardly carry the heavy bag strapped to her back. They had robbed Mr. Sowerberry's cash box and made their escape to the city. When they had found a small inn, *The Three Cripples*, Noah took the bag of money from Charlotte and they went inside.

Here the new couple talked about their robbery and their plans. A shaggy, red-headed old man, sitting at a nearby table, listened in as they talked. When he heard them discussing robbery, he joined them and let them know that they were all in the same line of work. And this is how Fagin met these two newcomers.

Fagin talked Noah and Charlotte into meeting with him the next day.

"Will ten o'clock tomorrow morning be all right?" he asked.

"Yes," they answered.

"And what shall I tell my good friends your *names* are?" Fagin asked slyly.

Noah smiled. "I am Mr. Morris Bolter. And this is Mrs. Bolter."

Mr. Claypole, now known as Mr. Bolter, moved into Fagin's house the very next afternoon after their meeting. The merry old gentleman then told Mr. Bolter the kind of "work" he did.

"We're all in this together, my dear," said Fagin. "You see, we all have the same threats hanging over our heads. I'm of the same importance to you—as you are to yourself. Just think, I know enough about you to put the noose round your neck!"

Noah put his hand to his throat. He said he agreed with Fagin, but he didn't sound as though he meant it.

"The hangman," continued Fagin, "the hangman, my dear, is a sad end. To keep my little business going, I depend upon you. It's this trust we have in each other that helps me get through the hard times." Here Fagin put on a sad face. "My best worker was taken from me just yesterday morning."

"Oh, you don't mean to say he died," Bolter said.

"Oh, no, not so bad as that."

"Then I suppose he was—" started Bolter.

"Wanted?" said Fagin. "Yes, he was wanted by the police."

"What for?" inquired Mr. Bolter.

"He was charged with trying to pick a pocket. They found a silver tobacco box on him—his *own*, my dear, his own." Fagin's face looked as though he were in pain. "And now, Mr. Bolter, I have a job for you…"

Bolter's first job was to go to court and find out what was going to happen to this "best worker"—The Artful Dodger.

Jack Dawkins shuffled into the courtroom. Taking his place in front of the judge, he asked why he was there.

"Silence there!" cried the jailer.

A policeman stepped forward to say that he had seen the prisoner try to pick the pocket of an unknown gentleman in a crowd. (Indeed, the Dodger *had* taken a handkerchief. But because it was a very old one, he had put it back again—but not before trying the handkerchief out for himself.) The policeman said the prisoner was searched and found to have a silver tobacco box.

"Have you anything to say at all?" said the judge, looking at the Dodger.

"I beg your pardon," said the Dodger, looking up. "Did you address yourself to me, my man?"

"I have never seen such an out-and-out young rascal, your Honor," said the officer. Then, he turned to the Dodger. "Do you have anything to say?"

"No," replied the Dodger, "not here. Besides, my attorney is having breakfast this morning with the Vice President of the House of Commons. I shall have something to say elsewhere."

"He's guilty!" shouted the judge. "Take him away."

"You'll pay for this, my fine fellers," roared Jack Dawkins. "I wouldn't let you set me free now if you was to fall down on your knees and beg me. Here, carry me off to prison! Take me away!"

CHAPTER SIXTEEN

Nancy's Fate Is Sealed

The Dodger was not the only prisoner. Nancy had become a prisoner of Bill Sikes. Ever since she had told everything to Rose Maylie, Nancy shook from fear most of the time. Bill saw this. One Sunday night, Nancy tried to go out to meet Rose at London Bridge, but Bill locked the door and held her down.

Fagin didn't trust Nancy either. He told Noah to follow her whenever she went out at night. When Fagin found out that she went to London Bridge on Sunday nights, he thought that sooner or later he would find out *why*. One Sunday night, Fagin told Noah to keep a sharp eye. He was sure they would find out something very soon.

By the light of the street lamps, Noah followed Nancy. He was careful, as always, to stay out of sight on the other side of the street.

As it happened, this same Sunday night Rose *did* come to meet Nancy under the lamplight on London Bridge. A fine old gentleman came with her.

"You were not here last Sunday night," said Mr. Brownlow.

"I couldn't come," replied Nancy. "I was held prisoner in my house."

"By whom?"

"By Bill Sikes who works for Fagin."

"You were not suspected *tonight*, I hope," asked the gentleman. "Do you think you're being followed?"

"No," replied the girl, shaking her head. "But it's not very easy for me to leave him unless I give him a sleeping potion."

"Does he wake up before you get back?" inquired the gentleman.

"No. He does not know what I'm doing. No one knows where I am."

"Good. Now Rose has told me your troubles and I believe your story," he said. "Our plans are

to track down this man, Monks, and find out what he knows. But if he cannot be found, you must lead us to that old man whom Bill Sikes and the others work for."

"Fagin!" cried the girl. "I will not do it! I will never do it!"

"Tell me why," said the gentleman.

"He *has* led a bad life… but I have led a bad life, too. There are many of us who have done the same things together. They have never turned against me, and I can never tell on them."

"Then," said the gentleman quickly, "let me take care of things. Tell me how I can find this man Monks—and *I* will deal with him."

"What if he turns against the others?"

"I promise you, we will protect your friends. But we have to find out what Monks looks like."

"He is tall," said the girl, "and he looks strong, but he is thin. He wears a black coat and hat and tries to hide his face. He has a slinking walk, and is always looking over his shoulder. The eyes"—Nancy shuddered—"they are sunk in deep in his pale face. He is a young man with dark hair—but he looks old. You'll know him by his very twisted mouth, and he often bites his lips. For you see, he has fits—"

Here, the gentleman and Rose became startled.

"One more thing," added Nancy. "Upon his throat, just hidden behind his handkerchief, there is a—"

"A broad red scar, like a burn?" asked the gentleman.

"You know him!" The young lady let out a cry of surprise.

"I think I do," said the gentleman. "Now, what can I do to help you?"

"Nothing," replied Nancy. "I am trapped in my old life. I have gone too far to turn back."

"Take this purse," insisted Rose.

"No!" replied Nancy. "I will take no money. But I would like to have something that belonged to you, sweet lady. A keepsake, perhaps?"

Rose handed her a silk handkerchief.

Nancy looked into the girl's face. "Bless you. Good-night."

The three figures left the bridge.

Noah Claypole—Mr. Bolter, that is—turned and ran for Fagin's house as fast as his bolting legs would carry him.

CHAPTER SEVENTEEN

Murder!

Early the next morning, Fagin sat huddled over a cold fireplace. He was boiling with anger. Noah had told him about Nancy's secret meeting. He could not wait to give Bill Sikes every detail.

The doorbell rang. It was Sikes, carrying a bundle of stolen goods.

"Come in, Sikes," said Fagin. "This man has something to tell you." He pointed a long thin finger at Noah sleeping in the corner. "Wake up, Bolter! Tell your tale again, about Nancy. You followed her?"

Noah rubbed his sleepy eyes. Bill's eyes filled with fire.

"Yes," said Noah slowly.

"You followed her to London Bridge?"

"Yes."

"Where she met two people?"

"Yes. She met a gentleman and a lady who asked her to tell about her friends. They wanted to know about Monks, too. She told them everything they wanted to know," Noah said.

"She did, did she?" cried Fagin, crazy with anger. "What did she say about *Sikes*?"

"She said she put a sleeping potion in his drink so she could get away from him and get outside."

Sikes had a wild, hateful look in his eyes. Rushing past Fagin, he ran from the room. He went straight to his own door. He opened it softly and went over to the bed where Nancy was lying. She raised up with a frightened, shocked look.

"Get up!" said Sikes.

"Bill," said the girl, in a scared, low voice, "why do you look like that at me? Bill, tell me what I have done!"

"You know!" hissed the robber. "You were followed and watched. Every word you said was heard."

"Then spare my life for the love of Heaven,

as I spared yours," begged the girl, clinging to him. "I never gave you away, Bill!"

Sikes got one arm free and grabbed his pistol. As poor Nancy looked up at him, he hit her head twice with the pistol, as hard as he could.

Nancy staggered and fell. She drew from her pocket a white silk handkerchief—the one Rose Maylie had given her. She held it up in her folded hands as high toward Heaven as her strength would allow. Then Nancy breathed one prayer for mercy.

Sikes, swaying back and forth like a wild animal, reached for a heavy club and brought it down hard. The girl fell to the floor and did not move.

Sikes could see Nancy's eyes and thought they were watching him. Sadly, he was wrong. Poor Nancy's eyes could see nothing. She was dead. Bill had murdered the only person who had ever cared about him.

He turned away from the bleeding body. Making sure no one had seen or heard anything, he whistled for the dog and quickly left.

But, as he left the city behind him, Sikes felt a fear begin to creep over him. He thought of those empty, glassy eyes he had just left.

Everywhere he looked, dead eyes seemed to be staring at him from the darkness.

Suddenly, he changed his plan and turned back toward London. "I'll find a good hiding place for a week or two—and then I'll go to France," he said to himself.

Then he remembered Bull's-eye. He couldn't have the mutt following him everywhere. Everyone—even the police—knew that Bull's-eye was his dog. This would give them one more thing to look for that could lead the police right to him. He decided to drown the dog and began looking around for a pond. He picked up a heavy stone as he went.

The animal looked up into his master's face. It was almost as though he knew what Sikes was planning. Bull's-eye lagged behind his crazed master, his head down and his tail between his legs. When Sikes stopped at a pool of water and called to the dog, Bull's-eye stopped and would not move.

"Did you hear me call? Come here!" cried Sikes.

The dog wagged his tail, but didn't move. Sikes started toward the dog, the big stone in his

hand. The dog looked at him for a few seconds,
backed away, and took off running.

CHAPTER EIGHTEEN

The Tale of Monks

At twilight, two men forced Monks into Mr. Brownlow's home, holding his arms tightly.

"For what reason am I kidnapped in the street and held here?" asked Monks. "This is strange treatment, sir," he said, throwing down his hat and cloak, "from my father's oldest friend."

"It is because of my friendship with your father," said Brownlow, "that you are not being treated much worse, *Edward Leeford*. Yes, I know your real name. I loved your father's sister and would have married her many years ago if she had not died. Your father and I cried together, and I never forgot him. It is just as well, Mr. Monks, that you call yourself by another name, for you do not *deserve* to have your father's name."

"This is all fine," sneered Monks, "but what do you want with *me*?"

"You have a brother," said Mr. Brownlow.

"I have no brother," replied Monks. "You know that as well as I."

"What I *do* know is that you are the child of a bad marriage. Your father, my closest friend, was forced by his family to marry your mother. It was just a business deal. He was never happy, and it tore at his heart until he could take no more."

"My parents split up," said Monks. "So what?"

"Your father found a chance for happiness. He moved to the country where he became friends with a naval officer, a Mr. Fleming by name. Mr. Fleming's wife had died and left him with two daughters. One was a beautiful girl of nineteen, and the other just a very young child. Your father and the older daughter fell in love and were engaged to be married."

"What's all this mean to me? Get to the point!" said Monks.

"Just before his wedding, a rich relative in Rome died and left your father a large amount of

money and property. He had to go to Italy to settle that business. Your mother heard about all this and went to Italy to find your father, taking you with her. She was a greedy, mean woman and was after any money she thought she might be able to get. Your father was sick when she arrived. He mysteriously died the next day. No legal Will was found, so all of his money and property went to you and your mother."

Monks said nothing.

"However, before he left for Italy, your father came to see *me*," said Mr. Brownlow slowly.

"I never heard of that!" said Monks, looking a bit worried.

"He left me a picture of the young woman he loved, which he himself had painted. He also told me that he planned to settle his affairs by giving your mother and you a *part* of his new fortune. Then he was to return from Italy, to marry the woman he loved. Of course, I never saw my good friend again. He never came back from Italy. I looked for the young lady whose face was in the painting. I wanted to help her in any way I could, but her whole family had moved away, and I never found her."

Monks sat back with a smile, looking much calmer.

Pulling nearer to Monks's chair, Mr. Brownlow continued. "*I* am the one who saved your little brother from a life of misery and crime. I took him into my home and gave the poor child the first good food and care he had ever been given. Of course, I had no idea who he truly was at that time. But while he was with me, I saw how much he looked like the young lady in the picture my friend had painted. I also noticed that he looked a great deal like my friend— Mr. Leeford—*your* father."

Monks began to squirm. His face became more twisted. Brownlow went on speaking.

"After your wicked friends stole Oliver from me, I could not help thinking how Oliver looked like that picture. I began to hunt *you* down to find the answers I wanted about your father. I went all the way to the West Indies, where I knew you had gone after your mother died. When I found you had left for London, I came back and have been looking for you ever since. Now, Edward Leeford—or should I call you Monks?—my search is over!"

"You—you can't prove anything against me!" cried Monks. "Just try it! I dare you! A painting of a lady whom you never found. Is that all? Ha!"

Mr. Brownlow moved closer to Monks and said he had not finished. He stared hard into Monks's face and went on.

"There *was* a Will, which your mother destroyed before she died. And she told you all about it. There was something in it about a child that was about to be born to your father and the woman he loved. This could be the only reason you have hunted the boy down. By a twist of fate, you recognized Oliver when you knocked him down in the street that day when I had my pocket picked. Did he look a little like your own father? Did you see something familiar in his face?"

Mr. Brownlow stopped a moment to calm his voice. "We know more. You destroyed proof of your brother's birth and who his parents were because you *knew* what was in the Will. And we also know that Fagin helped you. Who told us? A good-hearted girl—a kind soul who has been murdered for it." Mr. Brownlow's voice rose to a shout. "Now, Edward Leeford, your evil plans and schemes have brought Nancy a violent

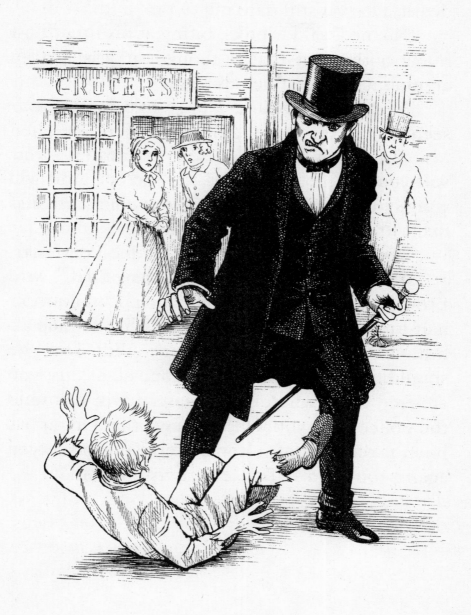

death. Do you still dare me to prove it?"

"No, no," said Monks, biting at his lips, "I—I knew nothing of that. I thought it was just an argument between her and Bill."

"No. It was because Nancy told part of *your* secret that the poor girl was killed," replied Mr. Brownlow. "You caused a murder! Now will you tell me the rest of the secrets? And will you sign a paper on which the whole truth has been written down?"

"Yes, I will do those things," mumbled Monks.

"You must do even more than that," said Brownlow. "You must give your poor, innocent half-brother, Oliver, everything that is due to him—everything your father's Will said he should have. When you have done all of this, you are free to go where you please. I will not send the police after you. Once I know that Oliver has been taken care of, I don't ever want to see you again. You are a selfish, evil, twisted man!"

CHAPTER NINETEEN

The End of Bill Sikes

Monks and the Dodger were not the only ones in trouble. Fagin and his ring of thieves were slowly but surely being found. Toby Crackit and another thief nervously discussed matters in Toby's attic hideout one night.

"When did the police pick up Fagin?" asked Toby.

"Just at dinnertime," said the other thief. "Bolter tried to hide in the empty water barrel. He dove in head-first, but his legs were so long that they stuck out at the top. So they grabbed him, too."

"And Charley Bates?" asked Toby.

"He'll be here soon."

"This isn't the end of all this," said Toby.

"The law will get more of us before it's done."

While the two sat trying to think what to do next, they heard a noise at the door. Bull's-eye leaped into the room. Toby went to the window, looked down, and saw Sikes coming their way.

"I hoped he wouldn't come here—but we've got to let him in," Toby said, picking up the candle.

Sikes came in looking like a ghost. His eyes were hollow and his face thin and white.

"How long's that dog been here?" he asked. "Was he alone?"

"Not long, and alone," said Toby.

"Tonight's paper says that Fagin's been captured. Is it true or a lie?" asked Sikes.

"True."

They were silent for a minute or two.

Then, turning to Toby, Sikes said, "Do you plan to give me up for a reward or let me hide out here until the police quit their manhunt?"

"You may stay here, if you think it safe," said Toby.

Sikes sat down across from the door. When Charley Bates entered, he looked straight at the big man. Charley's eyes widened in terror.

"Charley!" said Sikes, stepping forward. "Don't you know me?"

"Don't come near me," answered the boy, "you monster! You murdered Nancy!"

They looked at each other, then Sikes's eyes sunk slowly to the floor.

Charley screamed, "I'm not afraid of him. If they come here after him, I'll give him up. Murder! Help! Down with him!"

The boy attacked Sikes and knocked him down. The fight didn't last long. All at once, there was a loud knocking at the door and the sound of angry voices outside.

"Help!" shrieked Charley Bates. "He's here! Break down the door!"

"In the King's name, open up!" a voice shouted from outside. Soon more voices took up the cry. Some people tried to climb the wall. "Murderer! Murderer!" the mob screamed.

Sikes grabbed a rope and climbed through a window onto the roof. When the people saw him, a louder cry went up. Sikes looked down and saw hundreds of wild people screaming at him.

He saw only one chance to get away. He tied one end of the rope tightly around a chimney. With the other end he made a loop. Sikes brought the loop over his head in order to slip it under his

armpits and lower himself down. Just then, the murderer, looking behind him, threw his arms above his head and yelled out in terror.

"The *eyes* again!" he screamed.

His crazy mind snapped as he thought he saw Nancy's dead eyes watching him. Falling back in fear and shock, he slipped and tumbled over the roof's edge. The loop was around his neck. He fell for thirty-five feet to a sudden jerk! And there he hung—dead—swinging back and forth above the angry crowd.

Charley Bates called to the people below to come and take him away.

Bull's-eye had been hiding, but now he ran back and forth on the edge of the roof, howling. He jumped for the dead man's shoulders. Missing his aim, he fell and died on the ground below his master's swinging feet.

CHAPTER TWENTY

The Pieces Fall Together

Two days later, Oliver was in a carriage headed to the town where he was born. Mrs. Maylie, Rose, Mrs. Bedwin, and Dr. Losberne were with him. Mr. Brownlow followed in another coach. The others did not see that Brownlow traveled with a man—a tall, young man who was biting his lips.

As they passed familiar sights, Oliver thought of his little friend from the orphan work farm. "If only I could see Little Dick now!" he said.

"You will see him soon," replied Rose, gently taking his folded hands between her own. "You shall tell him how happy you are, and that you have come back to make him happy, too."

"Yes, yes," said Oliver, "and we'll take him away from here, where he may grow strong and well, shall we?"

They drove straight to a hotel where Mr. Grimwig met them. He was all smiles and kindness and did not offer once to eat his head. Mr. Brownlow did not join them at dinner.

When nine o'clock came, Mr. Brownlow entered the room with a strange man—*Monks!* Oliver cried out and almost fainted from shock. There was the cloaked man with the twisted face!

Monks threw a look of hate at the boy and sat down near the door. Mr. Brownlow, who had some papers in his hand, walked to a table near Rose and Oliver.

"This is a painful time," he said, "but these statements, which have been signed in London before many gentlemen, must be agreed to here—by this man." Brownlow turned to Monks. "Now, sir, was this boy here born to your father, my dear friend Edwin Leeford, and a lady named Agnes Fleming whom he was to marry? And did that poor lady die when this boy was born? And finally, is this boy, then, your half-brother and is your *real* name Edward Leeford and not Monks?"

Oliver gasped and cried out, "My brother?"

Monks stared at Oliver with dark, evil eyes. Turning back to Brownlow, he said, "What you have just said is true."

"Good," said Mr. Brownlow. "Now, will you read from your confession and tell us what else is true? And if you don't, you can be sure I will help you!"

"Listen, then," said Monks, and he began reading. "When my father became ill in Italy, he never came out of the coma he was in. My mother and I no longer lived with my father— but we were there when he died. Among his things, we found two papers addressed to Mr. Brownlow. They were to be sent to him only after my father's death. One of these was a letter to a lady, Agnes. The other was his legal Will."

"What was in the letter?" asked Mr. Brownlow.

"My father told her how much he loved her and asked for her forgiveness if he had caused her shame. He said if he had lived he would have been a good husband to her and a good father to their child that she was carrying. It also spoke of things he had given to her: a gold locket, which she was to wear next to her heart, and a gold

ring which would someday be engraved with his last name."

Poor Oliver began to cry. Rose put her arm around him.

"And the *Will*? What was in the Will?" asked Mr. Brownlow.

Monks was silent.

"You *know* what the Will said!" Brownlow shouted. "But if you won't speak, I will help you. The Will left you and your mother each some money to live on. But most of his fortune your father divided into two equal parts, one half for Agnes Fleming and the other for their child, if it should be born alive and grow to be of legal age. But the Will went on. It said that if that child were to become a lawbreaker—a criminal—then he would get *nothing*."

"My mother burned the letter!" cried Monks. "It never reached Agnes. My mother kept the Will and other proof so she could use it to hurt the Fleming family some day. Mr. Fleming moved away to Wales with his two daughters. He changed his name so his friends back home would never know about Agnes and her baby. The old man died before the child was born—

the shame killed him. Agnes, still pregnant, ran away from home."

Monks bit his lips. Mr. Brownlow continued, pointing at Monks. "Years after that, *this* man's mother came to me. She told me that her son, Edward, had left her when he was eighteen, robbing her of jewels and money. The mother was dying and wished to find her son. They got back together and went to live in France."

"My mother died there," said Monks. "On her deathbed she passed on these secrets to me. She believed a child had been born and lived, and would get half my money. I swore to her that I would hunt it down, and never let it rest. That child would never get any money my father left! I promised that I would try to have that child dragged to prison."

"Tell us about the locket and ring," said Mr. Brownlow, turning to Monks.

"I bought them from a man and woman who run a workhouse—they learned of them from an old, dying workhouse nurse. The nurse had taken them from that Agnes Fleming, who died when she gave birth to this boy here," answered Monks without raising his eyes.

There were more surprises in store.

Mr. Brownlow called out, "Mr. Grimwig, bring in Mr. and Mrs. Bumble!"

Pointing to Monks, Mr. Brownlow asked Mrs. Bumble, "Do you know that person?"

"No," she replied.

"I never saw him in all my life," said Mr. Bumble.

"You never sold him anything?"

"No," replied Mrs. Bumble.

Mr. Grimwig again left the room and returned with two old women who shook and tottered as they walked.

"You shut the door the night Old Sally died," said one of the women to Mrs. Bumble, "but you couldn't shut out the sound."

"That's right," said the other. "We listened to what she told you. And we followed you the next day when you took a piece of paper to the pawn shop."

"Yes, and we saw the man give you the locket and the gold ring. We were nearby."

"Would you like to hear more?" Brownlow asked Mrs. Bumble.

"No," Mrs. Bumble snapped. "I *did* sell that man the locket and ring, and now they're in the river where you'll never get them. So what?"

"I hope," said Mr. Bumble, "that this little thing will not cause me to lose my important job."

"Indeed it will," replied Mr. Brownlow.

"It was all done by *Mrs. Bumble*," the round man said as he left the room.

"Young lady," said Mr. Brownlow, turning to Rose, "give me your hand." He led her over in front of Monks. "Do you know this young lady, sir?"

"Yes," replied Monks.

"I never saw you before," said Rose faintly.

"I have seen you often," returned Monks.

"The father of poor Agnes had another daughter," said Mr. Brownlow. "What happened to the other child?"

"The child," replied Monks, "was sent to live with some country folk after the father died and Agnes left. From there, she was taken in by a widow woman who never knew the small child's true name or family. That child… is that girl in front of me—the one you call Rose."

"My darling Rose whom I called my niece!" cried Mrs. Maylie, holding the fainting girl in her arms.

"And she is my own dear aunt," cried Oliver, "whom I already love so much. Rose!"

CHAPTER TWENTY-ONE

Fagin's End

The courtroom was full on the day of Fagin's trial. The papers had reported the terrible life of crime he had led, and the people wanted to hear the facts for themselves. And hear them they *did*.

The jury was told all about his ring of pick-pockets, thieves, and murderers. They learned how he had ruined the lives of young boys by teaching them to steal and lie. The full story of Nancy's murder by Bill Sikes also came out. The jury heard that Fagin had paid and protected Sikes as one of his gang members.

Fagin was found guilty and sentenced to death by hanging.

A few days before the sentence was carried out, Mr. Brownlow took Oliver to see Fagin in his prison cell. Fagin was still the same wicked, mean person he had always been. In spite of this, and in spite of everything Fagin had done to him, little Oliver said a prayer for him.

Three days later, Fagin walked up the steps of the gallows. A noose was put around his neck. The hangman gave the final order, and justice was done.

CHAPTER TWENTY-TWO

How All Turned Out

Oliver's new start in life had one sad part. Little Dick had died. He never lived to see a better life. But Oliver never forgot him and how much Little Dick had loved him.

The property of Oliver's father was divided equally between his sons Edward and Oliver. Mr. Brownlow adopted Oliver as his son.

Edward went back to being Monks. He spoiled the second chance Mr. Brownlow had given him. He wasted all of his money and returned to crime. He died in prison.

Mr. Noah Claypole went free after ratting on Fagin. He went into business helping the police, which gave him and Charlotte enough money to get along.

Charley Bates, shocked by Sikes's crime, changed his ways. He moved to the country and found work on a farm.

The rest of Fagin's gang stayed in trouble with the law, and their lives ended in prison.

Mr. and Mrs. Bumble lost their jobs. When their money was gone, they were sent to live in that very same workhouse where they had once been so mean to others.

Mrs. Maylie's son, Harry, married Rose. They had a happy, loving marriage.

Mr. Grimwig never really ate his own head.

Mr. Brownlow loved Oliver more each day. He gave him books to study and showed him how to live a good life. Oliver never forgot to give prayers of thanks to the One from whom mercy and goodness comes. The love, hope, and peace that Oliver had searched for had finally come to him.

CHAPTER TWENTY-THREE

Treasures

In a town not named, near an old village church, there now stands a white marble gravestone. On it there is just one word—Agnes. Agnes—a young mother who gave her new baby boy one last kiss before she died. A young mother who gave an old nurse a locket, a gold ring, and one dying wish.

The gold treasures are lost forever at the bottom of a river somewhere in England. That doesn't matter. A mother's dying wish for her little boy's life came true. That's the treasure that matters—and lasts forever.

The End

The Flemings
Oliver's Grandparents

Rose Agnes' Sister	Agnes Fleming	♥ ♥ ♥	Edwin Leeford
Taken to Wales Father dies Adopted by Mrs. Maylie Renamed "Rose" and called Mrs. Maylie's niece	Dies in childbirth	Oliver Twist	Paints Agnes' portrait Dies in Italy

Work farm for orphans

Workhouse for the poor

Works for the Sowerberrys

Runs away to London
Joins Dodger and Fagin

Nabbed as a pickpocket

Lives with Mr. Brownlow

Bill Sikes and Nancy steal
him for Fagin

House is broken into	Breaks into a house
Takes care of injured Oliver	Is taken into the Maylies' home
Becomes ill and recovers	Attends to Rose when she's sick
Has a visit from Nancy Meets Nancy on London Bridge	Sees Mr. Brownlow on the street
Learns the truth	Learns of his true family
Finds out she is Oliver's Aunt	*Becomes Mr. Brownlow's Son*

180

The Leefords
Oliver's Grandparents

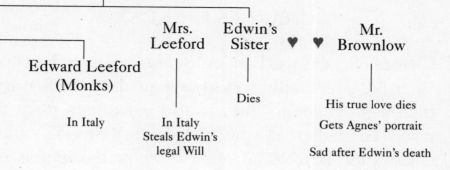

Edward Leeford (Monks)	Mrs. Leeford	Edwin's Sister ♥	♥ Mr. Brownlow
		Dies	His true love dies
In Italy	In Italy Steals Edwin's legal Will		Gets Agnes' portrait
			Sad after Edwin's death

Contacts Brownlow looking for Edward	Contacted by Mrs. Leeford looking for Edward
Dies	
Becomes "Monks"	
Recognizes Oliver on the street	Gets his pocket picked Thinks Oliver looks like portrait
Meets with Fagin to have Oliver kidnapped	
Tells Fagin about a house to rob	
	Goes to West Indies looking for Edward for information on Oliver, Edwin, and the portrait
Takes Fagin to spy on Oliver at Mrs. Maylie's house Meets the Bumbles and throws the ring and locket in the river	Returns to London
	Receives a visit from Rose and Oliver Meets Nancy on London Bridge
Nabbed by Brownlow Tells the truth	Nabs Monks Reveals the truth
	Adopts Oliver

CHARLES DICKENS

Charles Dickens was born in 1812 in Landport, Portsea, England. His family was always in debt, and—with their eight children—they had to move from place to place. His father was put into debtor's prison. Young Charles left school and came to know the horrors of poverty, child labor, and the workhouse system.

Through good fortune, the Dickens family came into a bit of money and Charles was able to go back to school. Later, he worked as a clerk for a lawyer, and then as a newspaper writer, reporting on court cases and the workings of the government.

Everything he had experienced, seen and learned went into his own stories, published in magazines as "Sketches by Boz." Dickens was an instant success. He went on to write short stories and novels that became widely famous, including *Oliver Twist* (1838), *A Christmas Carol* (1843), *The Cricket on the Hearth* (1845), *David Copperfield* (1850), *A Tale of Two Cities* (1859), and *Great Expectations* (1861).

Dickens' colorful characters, witty writing style, and surprising plots brought to light the conditions of the poor and helpless, and brought about changes to the laws throughout England. He was still working and actively writing up to his death in 1870.